THE
CONFESSIONAL

SUSPENDED

THE
CONFESSIONAL

Gabriel Goodman

MINNEAPOLIS

Darby Creek
A division of Lerner Publishing Group, Inc.
241 First Avenue North
Minneapolis, MN 55401 USA

For reading levels and more information, look up this title at
www.lernerbooks.com.

Front cover: © Tom Fullum/Getty Images (teen girl); Cover and interior: © iStockphoto.com/Sorapop (ripped paper).

Main body text set in Janson Text LT Std 12/17.5.
Typeface provided by Adobe Systems.

Library of Congress Cataloging-in-Publication Data

Goodman, Gabriel.
      The Confessional / by Gabriel Goodman.
           pages cm. — (Suspended)
      Summary: "Jenny Vang moves to a Wisconsin high school and, hoping to fit in, she posts a made-up story about a romance with a teacher on a secret message board called The Confessional" —Provided by publisher.
      ISBN 978-1-4677-5712-6 (lb : alk. paper)
      ISBN 978-1-4677-8099-5 (pb : alk. paper)
      ISBN 978-1-4677-8823-6 (eb pdf)
      [1. Rumor—Fiction. 2. Teacher-student relationships—Fiction. 3. High schools—Fiction. 4. Schools—Fiction. 5. Hmong Americans—Fiction.]
I. Title.
PZ7.G61366Co 2015
[Fic]—dc23   2014046177

Manufactured in the United States of America
1 – SB – 7/15/15

CHAPTER ONE

NOW
FRIDAY, OCTOBER 30

There were times when I'd look at my father and think: *This is the day. This is when the ogre within finally awakes.*

He gets this look where he closes his eyes and breathes in very slowly through his nose. He was doing that now. He was centering himself.

Dad has a terrible temper. Or so he'd always told me. I'd never seen it. He had never hit me, never yelled at me. But he'd raised me on stories of the anger he keeps inside—an awful ogre. "I do everything I can to keep it in, Jenny," he'd said a million times. When I was little, I totally bought that. Now that I'm sixteen, I think the ogre is just a metaphor.

Sitting in the school office next to Dad, I really, really hoped I was right.

Black-and-orange streamers hung everywhere, the closest thing the school had to Halloween decorations. A row of office assistants sat behind a waist-high wall, all of them typing away at their desktops. Or at least pretending to. Each assistant had flashed a look in my direction. And not one of those looks was sympathetic. They practically hated me.

I practically hated me.

Dad and I were waiting to get called into a meeting with the principal and other senior school staff. Two vice principals and some school board members. If anything was going to unleash Dad's hidden anger, this was it.

"Did you write the letter to Mr. Ashbury?" he asked me in the same soft voice he reserved for prayer.

I fished an envelope out of my bag. "I haven't had a chance to deliver it yet." Largely because I'm a huge chicken. I'd been really tempted to wait until Mr. Ashbury wasn't in his room, then throw it on his desk and run.

But, no. I had to look Mr. Ashbury in the eye when I gave it to him. It's an honor thing.

Dad's second-generation American Hmong. That means his parents came here straight from Laos. It also means he grew up in a household that stuck very rigidly to our culture's traditions. But he was the youngest of his siblings. Somehow those traditions didn't rub off on him. He allowed himself to be Americanized more than anyone else in the family. Dad didn't completely turn his back on where he came from. He just liked to pick and choose the things from our culture that meant something to him.

Just my luck, one of the things he'd chosen to keep was a strong sense of family honor. And since Dad didn't really talk to his parents or siblings anymore, our family was just him and me. And I think I threw that family honor in the toilet.

Dad didn't open his eyes. "Write it soon."

I nodded and shoved the envelope back into my bag. What I didn't say was, *That's if they let me anywhere near Mr. Ashbury when we're done here.*

Mr. La Clair, the principal's secretary, answered his phone. He muttered into the mouthpiece and hung up. "Mr. Vang, Jenny . . . Principal Boyle will see you now."

I gagged on a breath and turned it into a cough so no one would suspect how close I was to puking. But Dad knew. He opened his eyes and put his hand gently on my forearm. It was meant to be assuring. It was meant to tell me not to be afraid.

What it really told me is: do not fear the

ogre today. And that was what I really needed to hear.

We went down the hall to a small conference room. Principal Boyle, the vice principals, and two school board members crowded around the far end of a long table. Dad and I sat on the other end.

"Thank you for taking time off work to come in today, Mr. Vang," Principal Boyle said. I'm sure she said it just to make me feel guiltier. Which I didn't know was possible. "I won't take up too much of your time. As you know, we have a very serious situation. It's important that we send a clear message that this sort of thing won't be tolerated here at Monona High. We've talked about the best way to approach this and think we've come up with a fair solution."

Then Principal Boyle turned and looked directly at me.

"Jenny, you're being suspended for two months."

CHAPTER TWO

EIGHT DAYS EARLIER
THURSDAY, OCTOBER 22

Cough. Click!

Perfectly timed. I had to hand it to them. Shaniece and Abby—the girls who sat in front of me during American History—had their routine down. Shaniece knew just how to cup her hands and hide her cell phone while aiming its camera at the front of the room. And Abby knew just when to cough to hide the electronic *click* whenever Shaniece took a picture.

I leaned forward an inch, pretending to

be really interested in what Mr. Ashbury was teaching at the white board. I snuck a glance at Shaniece's phone when she flashed it at Abby, showing her their prize.

A picture of Mr. Ashbury in a rare pause.

Totally understandable. When he wasn't a whirlwind of teaching motion, pointing to maps and gesturing for effect, Mr. Ashbury was easy on the eyes.

Okay, he was hot.

I'd heard this was his first year teaching, making both of us new to Monona High. Mr. Ashbury didn't look any older than the rest of us. Piercing eyes behind hipster glasses, dark hair pointed in a faux hawk, chiseled jaw you could cut yourself on . . . No way was this the first time someone had taken a secret pic of him.

Abby cleared her throat. When I looked, she was glaring right at me. Shaniece caught me glancing at her phone and immediately pulled it close to her chest. Embarrassed, I went back to listening to Mr. Ashbury's lecture on the Bill of Rights. Not a good idea to upset the locals six weeks into the school year. If moving around a lot—eight schools in ten years—had taught me anything, it was to not make waves.

Once Shaniece was satisfied my eyes were off her, she stabbed at her phone's screen with her thumbs, typing furiously. A second later, the picture of Mr. Ashbury was uploaded under the caption *HOTTIE ALERT!* Before she slipped the phone back into her purse, I glimpsed the bright red banner of the site she was at.

The Confessional.

From what I knew about Shaniece, she wasn't the type to ask forgiveness for anything.

• • •

"What's the buzz?" Grant said, slamming down in the seat next to me. "Tell me what's-a happening."

Grant was an ambassador, one of the students the office assigns to show new kids around. Sweet guy, very helpful, took his job seriously. He popped up all over the place to make sure I wasn't feeling overwhelmed. He'd even tracked me down outside of school, like here at the West Towne Mall food court, where I'd come for a milkshake.

"It's nice of you," I said, "but you really don't have to check up on me so often."

"I took an ambassador's oath!" Grant said. "'Thou shalt not let the new girl feel alone.' I promise I'll stop in a few weeks. Until then, make this easy on yourself and tell me how it's going."

"Good," I said.

"Making friends? Meeting people?"

"Right now, I'm more worried about catching up." I pointed to the homework I was doing.

A second later, his two friends—DeShawn and Lia—sat down next to him. Grant and the rest of the drama club crew had adopted me. I wasn't sure if they genuinely wanted to be my friend or if they just needed someone to work backstage for the fall musical. I didn't have the heart to tell them that theater just wasn't my thing. Still, it was nice to have some insta-friends.

"Does anybody know," DeShawn asked, "why Shaniece Burton is throwing major shade this way?"

I followed his gaze to Shaniece, sitting two tables over and glaring right at me. No doubt about it. There might as well have been cartoon daggers coming out of her eyes.

"The death look would be for me," I said, trying to ignore her. "I think I saw something I wasn't supposed to." I didn't get why she was *still* mad. It's not like I was going to narc.

"What did you see?" Lia asked, hungry for gossip.

I sighed. "She uploaded a secret picture of Mr. Ashbury to some website and called him a hottie. The way she's staring, you'd think I killed her dog."

My friends went quiet. Grant looked sick and Lia looked scandalized.

"Was it The Confessional?" Grant said.

"That's the one."

Lia *oooohed* and fanned her face. "That's some hot stuff. No wonder she hates you, *chica*."

Hates me? For looking at her phone?

"Can we please change the subject?" Grant said, taking a drag on his Dr. Pepper.

"Ashbury is the new guy, right?" DeShawn said. "The pretty one? Sounds about right he'd be all over The Confessional."

"It's all the gossip you could want about anyone at Monona High," Lia said. "Who's dating who, who's having the most sex . . . you know, the basics. You want the dirt on anyone, that's where you find it."

DeShawn pulled out his phone and showed me the site.

"Looks like Reddit," I said.

DeShawn nodded. "Works the same way. Somebody posts a topic and then the comments start flying. You take it all with a grain of salt, but it can really open your eyes to the people you thought you knew."

I glanced over, and Shaniece was still glaring.

"Ignore that skizz," Lia said. She turned and gave Shaniece the finger. "She only goes to The Confessional for the attention. She loves to see everyone talk about all the guys she's hooked up with."

I was still learning the lingo at Monona. You could get in big trouble if anyone heard you use "the other s-word," the one that meant a girl who sleeps around. So everybody just said "skizz" instead. And when people talked about Shaniece, they said "skizz" a lot.

Grant rolled his eyes. "Way too gossipy for me. That place is toxic."

"You only think that because The

Confessional voted you 'Most likely to sleep with the Gargoyle for a lead role,'" Lia said, jabbing him in the ribs with her elbow.

The Gargoyle was what they called Mrs. Krause, the drama coach. I had her for Contemporary Lit. She was about as pleasant as her nickname suggested.

"Whatever," Grant said, rolling his eyes. "Really, Jenny, you don't want to go anywhere near that site."

"Got it," I said. But of course, I was really thinking, *I need to check this out.*

I'd never had any interest in being popular. Any time I'd ever changed schools, I was never the only new kid. It was easy to spot the others. I could see the ways they worked the system. They figured out who the most popular kids were and tried to worm their way in.

Not me. Just isn't who I am.

Now, fitting in—that's something completely different. Don't make waves. This was rule number one when trying to make friends at a new school. The second rule was to figure out the In.

The In was like a mass, shared interest. The one thing everybody (or almost everybody) talked about. Most schools, it was sports. Usually football, but not always. I'd develop a healthy-but-totally-fake interest in the In and pretty soon, I wasn't the outcast anymore.

Trash talk. That was the In at Monona High. Who knew?

CHAPTER THREE

SEVEN DAYS EARLIER
FRIDAY, OCTOBER 23

I'd promised myself that I'd finish all my homework before exploring The Confessional. And of course, *just* as I finished, and *just* as I was about to turn on my phone, the doorbell rang.

I glanced at the clock. 7:00. So much for The Confessional. I had a date. Well, an appointment.

When I crossed the living room to answer the door, Dad looked up from ESPN for the first time all night. He's the master of the Stone Face. Sad, happy, surprised—his expression never changes. But this time, when he looked at me with those blank eyes, I knew exactly what he was feeling: resigned.

"You don't have to do this, you know," he said.

"It's okay," I said. "I want to."

I opened the door to find another Hmong girl on the other side. She wore a plain white blouse and a navy skirt. Which kind of surprised me. I don't know what I was expecting, but it wasn't that.

"Mee?" I asked, even though I knew the answer.

Mee, the cousin I hadn't seen since I was six, nodded. "I was happy you called. It's so good to see you again, Jenny."

I was born in Madison. We moved away when I was six, right after my mom died and Dad decided he couldn't deal with the rest of his family anymore. Well, he always said it was for his job. But I knew the truth.

I was surprised when, after ten years away, he announced we were coming back here. I thought it was so he could make amends with his family.

I was wrong. My grandmother—Dad's mom—and the rest of the family hadn't even known we'd moved back until I called Mee. But when they found out, they hadn't really cared either. The bad feelings were mutual.

My family had been just me and Dad for a really long time. Ten years of moving, never really getting a chance to figure out who I was . . . I kind of wanted to know where I'd come from. So I reached out to Dad's family. Dad didn't stop me. But I knew he wasn't thrilled either.

"Are you ready to go?" Mee asked, pointing to her car.

"Do you want to come in? Say hi to my dad?"

Her smile disappeared. "No," she said, a little too quickly. "No, that's okay. We should get going."

Like I said: mutual bad feelings.

"Bye, Dad," I called back into the house. A second later, Mee and I were in her car and headed for the south side of Madison.

Words came out of Mee rapid fire. She told me about my cousins, my uncles, my grandmother. She shot through ten years of family history in about ten minutes. When I got a chance to speak, I quizzed her on the kind of music she listened to, her favorite movies. We had a lot in common.

"It's too bad we go to different schools," I said. "We could hang out more."

"We'll find lots of time to hang out. Grandmother will insist you visit as often as you can."

"Really?" I was kind of worried that I'd been written off, like Dad. Sure, the family had taken my call. Sure, Mee had invited me over. But for all I knew, she and the others were going to sit me down and tell me how horrible I was for abandoning them. Which I think is what Dad was expecting.

"Grandmother will be so happy to see you," she said.

I nodded. "I tried to get Dad to give her a call, but—"

"That's probably not a good idea," she said.

We pulled up to a small white house on Fish Hatchery Road.

"In fact," she said, taking a deep breath, "you might not want to mention your dad at all."

"Why?" I asked. "Do you know why those two don't get along? He's her son."

Mee shook her head. "No. She doesn't see it that way. He's dead to her."

I opened my mouth to respond, but she shook her head again. "It's great that you reached out to us. Grandmother wants you to be part of the family."

When Mee said that, my stomach did a somersault. Like it was something I'd wanted to hear but hadn't known I wanted. Every new school, I'd tried to belong. Maybe this was what I really wanted: just to fit in with my own flesh and blood.

We walked up a crooked path to the house. I followed Mee's lead and slipped my shoes off on the porch before we went in. As soon as we were through the door, the overpowering smell of curry and coconut hit me. My eyes started to water.

"Have you had dinner?" Mee asked.

I nodded. But still, the food smelled great. It reminded me of when Mom used to make curry. Dad never did.

A small woman in a red-and-gold dress emerged from the kitchen. Even though my memories of her had faded, I knew this had to be my grandmother.

She smiled and chattered in Hmong. I smiled back and said quietly to Mee, "I don't speak—"

"She says she's very happy to see you," Mee said.

"It's good to see you too," I said. Mee translated.

Grandmother took my hand and continued to chatter in this language I should have understood but didn't. She led me into the kitchen, where a number of men sat around a table, eating. I guessed they were my uncles and cousins. Women—aunts and other cousins—scurried around, preparing various dishes.

I'd forgotten: in traditional Hmong homes, the men ate before the women. It was kind of weird to see. Dad and I always ate together.

"—And you can take some home."

I hadn't realized that Mee had been translating Grandmother's constant talking.

"Sorry, what?" I asked.

"There's plenty of food," Mee repeated, "and you can take some home. Grandmother insists."

Grandmother spoke loudly over everyone at the table. They all looked up and broke out into smiles. Those who spoke English, which was just about everyone, said "hello" or called out my name.

Grandmother patted my hand and all but forced me into a chair. She spoke again.

"You're home," Mee told me.

And the weirdest thing of all: it felt like she was right.

CHAPTER FOUR

Home alone on Saturday night, I laid back on my bed, phone in hand, scrolling through Confessional discussion threads. The newest topics ranged from fairly tame—*Which teacher would you banish from planet Earth?*—to far racier stuff—*Who is the nastiest cheerleader?* The racy stuff way outnumbered the tame stuff.

Nastiest cheerleader. Skeeziest soccer player. Some senior named Wade Daniels had his own thread. It was filled with pictures of him on the football field, on the wrestling mats, and even one pic from behind, supposedly taken in the locker room shower. Wade himself chimed in, saying he couldn't confirm if that butt shot really was him. But he also said he couldn't deny it.

A number of girls who claimed to have slept with him were more than happy to vouch for the butt.

I spotted Shaniece's *HOTTIE ALERT* about Mr. Ashbury. When I clicked on it, I found that lots of people had added their own snapshots: pics of him walking down the hall, sitting at his desk, getting out of his car in the parking lot. It was like a creepy ode to his beauty.

One of the pictures was black and white: a yearbook portrait of Mr. Ashbury in a wrestling singlet from about six years ago, when he attended Monona High.

"He went to Monona?" I said to myself. "No way . . ."

In between each picture, everyone was guessing if he was single. At the bottom of the screen, a live chat window ran through the latest comments. Everyone used a fake name, but most of their avatars gave them away.

TheQueen: no way something that tasty is single LOOK AT THOSE PECS!!

This was Ashley Peterson. Her avatar was the picture of her being named Homecoming Queen last year. The same picture in the display case at school. Why bother with the fake name?

MissThang: check his finger. no ring

My new bestie: Shaniece. Her avatar was a close-up of a raised middle finger. I only knew this was her because MissThang had started the thread and posted the picture of Ashbury.

HannahBanana: i heard his girlfriend teaches at madison north

No clue who this was. I'm guessing one of the four thousand Hannahs who went to Monona.

TheQueen: i wonder if he's available after school to give "extra credit."

MissThang: he won't sleep with you ashley. you too nasty.

TheQueen: you think he'd sleep with you?

HannahBanana: you could ask him ashley. he's probably sloppy seconds after shaniece

Well, I thought, *I wanted to fit in.* And maybe if I joined in, Shaniece would stop glaring at me from across the cafeteria. She'd know she could trust me to be quiet the next time she snapped a picture. And if I wanted her to know it was me, I couldn't use a fake name. So I logged in and typed a response.

JennyV: Been there, hit that.

Nobody responded. Instead, one by one, I watched the girls all log out. Great. Now Shaniece was probably going to glare at me for daring to butt into her chat. I couldn't win with her.

I spent a couple more hours sifting through the threads. I got the feeling DeShawn was right. Most of this stuff *had* to be made up, like me hinting that I'd slept with Mr. Ashbury. I couldn't figure out what I'd done to offend the others. *Probably jealous*, I decided. They wanted to fantasize about Mr. Ashbury on their own.

He's mine, girls, I thought. *In Fake Boyfriend Land*.

I heard a knock at my bedroom door, just before Dad poked his nose in.

"Done with homework?" he asked.

"Did it last night."

He shook his head. "They didn't give you enough for the whole weekend? Teachers are a bunch of slackers these days."

I threw my pillow at him and got a rare smile. "There's some curry in the fridge. Got it from Grandmother. Help yourself."

Sure enough, that's all it took to invite back the Stone Face. "How did that go?" His face might have been a mask, but his voice told me just how curious he was.

"Great. Fine. I like Mee. We're going to study together next week."

Dad leaned on the door frame. "At my mother's house?" *Ladies and gentlemen, meet the man who can frown with just his voice.*

"Yeah," I said. "Is that a problem?"

He stood there a long time, taking this in. Then he nodded. "Okay. If that's what you want."

I put my phone down. "So, I know deep, meaningful talks aren't really our thing . . . but are you ever going to tell me why you hate your family so much?"

"I don't hate them. We just don't always . . . agree."

"They seemed pretty nice."

"I'm sure they did." Then he tilted his head toward the living room. "Wanna stream a movie?"

Dad could change a subject with the stealth of a lion on the hunt. I got up. He worked so much, it was rare when we got a chance to just sit and chill. "Sure. But don't think this means I'm going to stop asking what your beef with the family is."

"Honestly, Jenny," he said, Stone Faced and sad-voiced, "I really hope you never find out."

CHAPTER FIVE

FOUR DAYS EARLIER
MONDAY, OCTOBER 26

Monday was like the slowest train wreck in the history of the world.

I should have seen it coming. I'd been at the school two weeks, and no one had given me a second glance. Monday, all eyes were on me. Some people tried to hide it, glancing at me from behind books. Others just outright stared. I'm guessing the looks continued after I went past because of the whispers and giggles that followed me.

First period—Calculus—I glanced over at Glenn, the guy across the aisle from me. The top page of his notebook said *EASY* in big letters with an arrow pointing right at me. When I raised an eyebrow at him, trying to ask what it meant, he just laughed and licked his lips.

Then homeroom—Contemporary Lit with the Gargoyle. Every time Mrs. Krause buried her nose in her copy of *The Chocolate War* and read aloud, random guys would turn to face me and waggle their tongues. None of the girls even bothered to look at me.

When I got to history, the first thing I noticed was Mr. Ashbury wasn't there. The sub told us to take out our books and read chapters seven and eight. It was the most normal class I had all day. Until the bell rang. The sub hightailed it out, and when I tried to leave, two guys in football jerseys blocked my way.

"Hey, new girl," the taller one said. "We heard you like jocks."

Everyone else was moving past us and out the door. "What?" I said. "I think you've got the wrong—"

"Are you why Ashbury isn't here today?" the shorter one asked. "Is he too sore?"

Just then, Shaniece stepped in between me and the football guys. She looked the tall one right in the eye. "If she is, it's none of your damn business."

The guys laughed and left. Before I could say anything, Shaniece grabbed her bag and walked away. With only five minutes between classes, I didn't have a lot of time. I ran through the halls until I found Grant, DeShawn, and Lia next to Grant's locker.

"Guys," I said, "the weirdest thing just—"

That's when I noticed them all looking at me like I'd grown a third eye.

"Chica," Lia said, "we heard."

"About Shaniece standing up for me?"

DeShawn shook his head. "No. About you . . . and Mr. Ashbury."

Grant won't even look at me. He just keeps fumbling with the lock on his locker. "I told you to stay off that site."

I couldn't believe it. *That's* what this was all about?

"You're kidding, right?" I asked. "The Confessional is full of people bragging about who they hooked up with. Why am *I* getting all the attention?"

Grant groaned. "You need to know about some recent history. Last year, there was a big scandal. Mrs. Reynolds, the algebra teacher, was fired for sleeping with a student. It made national news. She's in jail now."

"Did you really sleep with Mr. Ashbury?" Lia asked, her face dead serious.

"Of course not!" I said. "Everyone was talking smack. I just joined in."

"Well, I heard the police escorted Ashbury out of school this morning," Lia said.

What? "That's crazy. The police should check out The Confessional. Everybody was saying stuff like that."

DeShawn shook his head. "Nuh-uh. They all talk about sleeping with *each other*. Nobody else was claiming to sleep with a teacher. That was all you."

I slumped against the lockers. "What do you think they'll do to Mr. Ashbury?"

Grant shrugged. "If what you said is true and nothing happened, they'll let him go."

Two girls from Calculus passed by, looking at me and snickering.

"Great. In the meantime, everyone thinks I'm the class skizz."

"Don't worry," Lia said, patting my arm. "You'll never be the class skizz as long as Shaniece Burton will do it with anything that moves."

Was that why Shaniece drove the jocks away? She was grateful I was taking the heat off her?

"Besides," Grant said, trying to sound optimistic, "you didn't do anything. You're fine."

"Jenny Vang," the loudspeaker nearby croaked. "Jenny Vang, please report to the office."

We all looked at each other. "It's a coincidence, right?" I asked. "It has nothing to do with . . . you know."

Grant shrugged. "Only one way to find out."

* * *

Two police officers were waiting in the principal's office. My first thought was Dad. He'd been hurt at work or something. But the officers' faces weren't sympathetic, like they were about to break bad news. They looked ready to haul me off to Alcatraz.

"Jenny," Principal Boyle said. "We've gotten a report about something you posted on a website this weekend. Something about Mr. Ashbury."

I felt my face flush. If I'd had lunch already, I probably would have lost it. "No, it wasn't . . . I just . . ."

Boyle raised her hands. "It's okay. We just need you to tell us the truth. You won't be blamed if Mr. Ashbury—"

"Nothing happened!" I blurted out.

One of the officers—a woman with blonde hair done up in a bun—scribbled onto a note pad. "You're saying you didn't have sex with your teacher?"

"Yes," I said. My cheeks were burning. "Is Mr. Ashbury okay? I heard he was taken from school."

The other officer—a guy in a tan trench coat—leaned across the principal's desk. I think he was trying to be comforting, but it came across as creepy. "Are you saying nothing happened because he threatened you?"

I started crying. I told them everything. That I made it up just to fit in. That I was still a virgin. Most of all, I repeated over and over and over that Mr. Ashbury and I never hooked up.

Principal Boyle and the police officers looked to one another for a long time. Finally, the principal said, "Jenny, we called your father and asked him to come pick you up. You should probably go home while we talk about this."

I wanted to die. What had they told Dad? As if she could read my mind, Boyle said, "He doesn't know about this. Yet."

I felt a bit of relief. "Am I in trouble?"

But no one answered. Instead, they asked me a few more questions. The whole group was trying really hard to make sure Ashbury hadn't threatened me not to tell anyone about our love affair that never happened. Then they let me wait outside for Dad.

He showed up a few minutes later. I muttered that I felt sick, and we walked to the car.

He didn't ask any questions. He just drove me home. I went to the bathroom and threw up.

CHAPTER SIX

Listening to Grandmother speak was like magic.

Mee and I had spread our school books across Grandmother's kitchen table. But I couldn't focus on homework. Grandmother was telling me stories about life back in Laos as my dad's brother, Uncle Ger, translated.

"You're kidding!" I said, amazed. But Uncle Ger said it was true: Grandmother worked for the CIA during the Vietnam War. That sounded cool. My grandmother, the spy.

Every so often, Uncle Ger would stop to teach me some words in Hmong. He taught me how to say *grandmother*: "niam pog." Her eyes lit up when I spoke her native tongue.

After an hour, Mee chased Grandmother and Ger away, saying we had homework to do. Grandmother left the room, grinning like a devil.

"I can't believe I didn't know that about her," I said, turning back to my books.

"Grandmother's an amazing woman," Mee said. Then she eyed me closely. "So . . . are you feeling okay? When your dad answered the door, he said you were sick and might not be able to study."

I tried to picture that uncomfortable scene: Dad answering the door when Mee showed up. I was surprised he'd said anything at all to her. I wondered if she'd spoken to him.

"Just a stomach bug yesterday," I said. "I'm good now, thanks."

Throwing up the day before had turned

out to be a good thing. It convinced Dad I was sick, and he insisted that I stay home. Which was fine with me, because I didn't want to face anyone at school. I figured this would give them time to verify with Ashbury that nothing had happened and then everything would go back to normal. Almost everything. When I came back to school on Wednesday, I wouldn't be the class skizz anymore. I'd be the class liar.

I could live with that.

Mee smiled brightly. "Whew. I couldn't tell if you were sick or if . . . something else was bothering you." When she brought up "something else," she quickly looked down at her notebook.

"No, it's all cool," I said. "Thanks for asking."

She buried her nose in the notebook but kept sneaking glances my way. It got to the point where I wanted to make sure I didn't have *FREAK* tattooed on my forehead. After the tenth sneaky glance, I said, "How about you? Everything okay?"

Mee swallowed hard and tucked her hair behind her ear. "No. Not really. I mean, I don't know."

"What is it? School problems? Boy problems? Girl problems?"

"Listen, I hate to ask this. I feel stupid but . . . Well, there's this rumor going around my school. A rumor about you."

I felt my stomach demanding an encore of yesterday's vomit attack. Mee went to school on the other side of Madison. How did anyone there know about all this stuff with The Confessional?

"It's not true," I said quickly, not looking up from my calculus. "None of it. It's just . . . it's just stupid."

Mee sighed. Her shoulders slumped and she sat back. "I'm so glad to hear that. I'll tell Grandmother."

"What?"

Mee shook her head. "No, I mean, if it

comes to it. You see how fast the rumor spread from one school to the next. I figure it's only a matter of time before the rumor makes the rounds at the Hmong Community Center. Grandmother's got friends who work there. They tell her *everything*."

I was *just* getting to know my family. The last thing I needed was for them to think bad things about me. Why hadn't I said I'd slept with Wade Daniels like everyone else?

"Don't worry," Mee said, taking my hand. "I can head off any trouble. I'll explain to her it was a lie someone started to make you look bad. She'll be angry *for* you, not *at* you."

I managed a meek smile. I wanted to correct her. It wasn't a rumor *someone* started. *I'd* started it. By accident (sort of). But if I was lucky, this would all blow over soon. People would stop talking about it. Maybe the rumor would die before it ever made it to Grandmother.

"Thanks, Mee," I said. "That means a lot."

"We're family," she said. "You don't know what that means yet. I hope you'll give us a chance to show you."

I'd spent the day in my room, trying to figure out how I could show my face at school on Wednesday. With Mee standing up for me, it suddenly felt very doable. Screw trying to fit in with a bunch of strangers. I had a family. Finally. That seemed more important than getting anybody at Monona to like me. I liked Mee. I'd always wanted a sister. But a cousin would do just as well.

"You know," I said, "maybe I could come with you to the Hmong Community Center sometime. I just feel like . . . I'm missing out on something, you know? I want to know more about our culture."

You'd think I'd just given her a million dollars. She squealed. "Grandmother will be so happy to hear that," she said.

* * *

When I got home, I found Dad waiting in the living room.

"You didn't have to wait for me," I said, slinging my backpack in the corner.

"Is something going on at school?" he asked.

My heart jumped up into my throat. As usual, Dad was calm. He could just as easily have been asking if I'd had a good evening.

"Why?" I asked.

My mind raced. Had he found The Confessional himself? I wished more than ever that I'd used a fake name online.

"I got a call from school after you left with Mee," he said. "They want me to come in for a meeting on Friday."

CHAPTER SEVEN

At school the next morning, I headed straight to the office. The person who called Dad had told him to give me those instructions. Apparently, the caller hadn't told Dad what this was about. The administrators were "still assessing the matter" and couldn't comment. And I couldn't tell Dad because *I* didn't know. They *must* have confirmed with Mr. Ashbury by now that it was all a lie. We'd never had sex. And since practically every student at school lied on The

Confessional about the sex they were having, how could I possibly be in trouble?

But when I got to the office, Principal Boyle took me behind closed doors.

"What you said online caused a big stir, Jenny," she said. Nothing about her tone was friendly. "Parents are calling me. The school board's getting involved."

"I already told you: it was a lie." I gripped my backpack handle tight to keep my hands from shaking. "I made it up. Ask Mr. Ashbury."

Boyle raised an eyebrow. "A lot of people are upset. Something like this has happened at Monona before."

I nodded. "I heard. But that guy actually had sex with the teacher."

"And the teacher got fired."

I dropped my backpack. "Did Mr. Ashbury get . . . fired?" I already felt miserable. I didn't think I could handle finding out a teacher had lost his job over me.

She scribbled onto a hall pass and handed

it to me. "Everything is still being discussed. Until this matter is resolved, you're to report to in-house detention. And it's best if you not go anywhere near Mr. Ashbury."

I glared at the hall pass like it might sting me. I'd never gotten a detention in my life. "This doesn't make sense. We didn't have sex. I admitted I lied. Why is this still an issue?"

Boyle's cheeks puffed up. I could see anger in her eyes. "We take student-teacher relationships very seriously here. Even if you didn't sleep with Mr. Ashbury, you've embarrassed him by letting people think you did. Maybe you should think about that."

She opened the door and wouldn't even look at me as I walked out.

. . .

The in-house detention room was just outside the office. Mr. Parker, the school aide, sat at a desk at the front, reading a newspaper. Half a dozen guys and girls—ones that I had regularly seen sitting in this room when I passed by—looked me up and down. The ones that recognized me whispered to the rest. Soon they were all smiling and chuckling.

Shaniece Burton sat in the far corner, away from everyone else, doodling in her notebook. Her eyes flashed for a second when she saw me. I thought I was in for more death glares. But instead, she went back to her notebook. I took a desk somewhere between her and the regulars and worked on my English report.

Two class periods came and went. As third hour was starting, Mr. Parker got up out of his chair. "Stay here," he ordered. "I'll be right back."

As soon as he left the room, the regulars burst out laughing.

"Ten o'clock, every day!" a boy named Todd Long said. "He must have his bladder set up to an alarm."

The girl next to him, whose name I didn't know, turned in her seat and faced me. "So . . .

you and Mr. Ashbury, huh? You know how to pick 'em."

I bit my lip. "It wasn't like that," I said quietly. "I didn't . . ."

"So will you do anybody?" another guy, Tim Harley, asked, grabbing his crotch.

"Of course she will!" Todd answered. "She's a big old skizz, aren't you?"

"Got a lot of experience spotting a skizz, Long?"

We all turned to look at Shaniece. It was nice to see her death glare aimed at somebody else for a change.

Todd's friends burst out laughing. A second later, Shaniece was on her feet. I swear I saw Todd jump a little.

"You think *this* little thing was with Ashbury?" Shaniece asked. "Please. Her V-card ain't been punched yet. But you know what? Even if she had done it, that's her business. Sleeping with somebody doesn't make a girl a skizz."

I must have sat there with my jaw dropped for a minute. Twice now, Shaniece had stood up for me. She'd wanted me dead last week.

The girl next to Todd folded her arms. "Says the skizz."

I was no expert in body language, but everything about Shaniece told me she was seconds away from leaping across the room and gouging out everyone's eyes. "What, because I've had sex?" Shaniece said, "That makes me a skizz, huh? Like that big skizz Wade Davis?"

"He's a guy," Todd said. "That's different."

Shaniece laughed. "Oh, *please* use that 2.0 GPA to tell me what the difference is."

Todd jumped up just as Mr. Parker came back.

"Siddown," Parker said. Then he looked at Shaniece. "All of you."

When Todd looked ready to protest, Parker said, "You just got back from a three-day suspension for punching the captain of the football team, Long. You can't afford any more black marks. Do you really want to push me? Everyone. Sit. Down."

Everyone did as they were told. The rest of the day went by without anyone saying a single word.

* * *

When the final bell rang, we were excused. On the way out, I tapped Shaniece on the shoulder.

"Thank you," I said, not knowing what else to say. "You didn't have to do that."

"Do what?" she asked. "Live my life? Welcome to what I deal with every day. I'm only sorry you had to find out what it's like. Just remember: there's no such thing as a skizz. It's your body. No one can make you feel ashamed for what you choose to do."

She sounded a little sad. I'd heard so many people call Shaniece a skizz—to her face and out of earshot—that it never occurred to me that it might hurt. Maybe it didn't. Maybe she was just sad for me.

"See you here tomorrow," I said.

"This was just a one-day trip for me," she said. "You're in here tomorrow too? Please tell me this doesn't have to do with Ashbury."

I nodded.

"Damn! For lying? That ain't right. You didn't do anything!"

"I embarrassed Mr. Ashbury. And I guess parents are angry."

Shaniece slung her purse over her shoulder. "They're putting you in detention for not doing anything. Imagine what they'd do if you did something." She leaned in close. "If this doesn't go away fast, *you* might wanna get angry."

As Shaniece walked away, I imagined what it would be like to have a fiery ogre inside, just like Dad. Yeah, that was never going to happen. Besides, Shaniece had said I didn't do anything. But I did. I'd lied. I deserved a couple days in detention. *It could be worse*, I thought.

That was right before it got *a lot* worse.

CHAPTER EIGHT

I found out when I got home from my first day of in-house detention that the police had stopped by our house to bring Dad up to speed. If I had known that when I sat in detention, I would have spent the day throwing up.

Dad didn't say a word to me all through dinner. Didn't even look at me. We went to bed without speaking.

The next morning, I couldn't take it anymore. As we sat down to breakfast, I said,

"I'm going over to Mee's tonight to study." Dad's big meeting with the principal—no, *our* big meeting—was tomorrow. I desperately needed to spend time with my cousin and cry or laugh or do whatever it is you do with cousins who want to comfort you when you're upset. At least, that's what I hoped Mee would do.

"You're not going out," Dad said, finishing his coffee. "You're grounded for a week."

"For lying online?"

"For lying to me," he said. "You told me you didn't know what this meeting was about. If you'd told me the truth . . ."

"It was embarrassing. I didn't think it would lead to this. I was hoping it would go away."

"Well, it didn't. And now you have to deal with the consequences. Part of that is being grounded."

"That's not fair," I said. "I didn't lie to you. I really didn't think it would go this far. How was I supposed to know?"

"You still should have told me. The school didn't say what was happening because even they didn't know where this was going. But Mr. Ashbury considered pressing libel charges—"

"He what?" This was getting crazier by the minute.

Dad raised a calming hand. "He's decided *not* to. But obviously you won't be in his class anymore. I'm sure that's just the start of what the school wants to do. All I'm doing is punishing you for lying about something where the police were involved. No seeing Mee for one week."

So *that's* what this was about. It was an excuse to keep me from his family. My family. He didn't care that I'd lied to him. He'd just been waiting for something he could use to keep me away from Grandmother and Mee.

"Look," I said, "I already admitted that what I did was stupid. I'm never going to do anything like that again. I won't lie about sex

I didn't have on the Internet. I won't lie to you when the police are involved. But punishing me because I was trying to fit in—"

"You don't need to fit in!" Dad said. I'd never heard him come so close to actually yelling. "You need to do your homework, get good grades, and stay out of trouble."

But even if he wouldn't yell, there was nothing stopping me. "I *do* need to fit in! I don't have anything else. You've kept me from my family. You've dragged me all around the country because you can't stop running from them. Now we're finally home with aunts and uncles and cousins, and I'm *still* alone."

Dad flinched. All our lives, we'd only ever argued a few times. He'd won every argument. I couldn't help but think, for once, I'd made a point he couldn't fight.

Even so, he didn't back down. "One week. If you push, it's one week without your phone too."

That's when I knew exactly how serious

this was. He'd gone for the nuclear option. Dad had never threatened to take away my phone. Or anything, really. But now he was hitting right where he knew it would do the most damage. He knew there was no way I'd speak up any further.

I threw my gaze across the room, looking at anything that wasn't him. I made silent plans to sneak out of the house and meet up with Mee. I was sure Grandmother would be angry at Dad with me. Maybe she'd break her ten years of silence and call him up just to chew him out about grounding me.

Dad cleared his breakfast plates and straightened his tie.

"And while you're in detention today," he said, grabbing his briefcase, "you're going to write a letter to Mr. Ashbury and apologize for what you said."

As soon as the door closed behind him, I threw my orange juice glass into the sink and enjoyed the sound of it smashing.

● ● ●

Shaniece wasn't in detention that day. I sat in her seat, far away from Todd and the other regulars, and opened up my notebook. I wrote: *Dear Mr. Ashbury, I'm sorry I didn't sleep with you. Maybe this all would be worth it if I had.*

I ripped that page to shreds. The last thing I needed was for someone to think I meant that. Even if I did a tiny bit.

I didn't know what to say. Mr. Ashbury had been a wrestler. Was I really supposed to believe that he'd never boasted about something that wasn't true?

Dear Mr. Ashbury, Have you ever not fit in? Do you know what that's like? Probably not. You were a wrestler and they tend to be popular. Well, I said what I said because I was trying to fit in. I didn't think it would hurt anyone. Did it really hurt you? Well, it's hurting me.

I tore that one up too. It sounded whiney.

Dear Mr. Ashbury, Were you really going to press libel charges?

By the time Mr. Parker walked us down to the cafeteria for lunch, I'd written ten apology letters, all of which I'd destroyed. I wasn't sure there was anything I *could* say.

For the rest of the day, all I could focus on was how angry I knew Dad was. How disappointed. I'd been mad at him when he grounded me. But the fact was that I was in major trouble. He was probably embarrassed at having raised a kid who was causing this much of a scandal.

Maybe I deserved whatever they were planning to do to me.

CHAPTER NINE

NOW
FRIDAY, OCTOBER 30

"Jenny, you're being suspended for two months."

Two months? That was insane. That was *beyond* insane. Todd Long had only gotten a three day suspension and he'd decked a guy. How could a lie be worse than physical violence?

I'd been ready for Dad to just nod and agree and, boom, it would all be over. But he didn't.

"I've spoken with the police about this at length," Dad said. "Jenny said she did something that she didn't do. The police agree that she didn't do it. From what I understand, Mr. Ashbury confirms it too, and he's not pressing charges."

Principal Boyle blinked. That was *not* the reaction she'd been expecting. "Students at Monona are all held to a code of conduct. Everyone: athletes, honor students, student council members. What Jenny did was a violation of that code."

"How, exactly?"

That's when I almost started crying. As angry as he was, Dad still defended me. Even he knew two months was unfair.

Boyle shifted in her seat, very uncomfortable. In fact, everyone on her side of the table looked like they were standing on a hot plate and someone had just turned the heat up.

"Not everyone knows Mr. Ashbury has been cleared in all this," the principal said, avoiding Dad's question. "Parents are still calling me, asking Mr. Ashbury to be removed from his classroom. Jenny's actions embarrassed a good teacher and created an administrative nightmare for me."

"And that merits a *two-month* suspension?" Dad was cooler than cool.

One of the men behind the principal—a guy in a gray suit with thinning hair—spoke up. "Yes. The school board discussed this last night in an emergency meeting, and we think this is fair."

"Fair," Dad said, "would be punishing the other students on that website who also boasted about sex."

It was all I could do not to *whoop* with excitement. I'd been ready to walk out and accept the suspension. But Dad made me want to fight back.

Gray Suit practically sneered at Dad. "If Jenny isn't punished, other students will think it's okay to make similar claims. We'd spend all our time fending off lawsuits and conducting interviews and sorting out who did what with whom. You should know that we'd originally discussed *expulsion*. I'm sure you agree this solution is much better."

Dad sat quietly for a very long time. So long that even I became as uncomfortable as the suits he was staring down. There was ice in those eyes. Then he stood. "No. I don't agree." Without another word, he turned and walked out. I jumped up to follow but, before I did, I turned back and smiled.

"Thank you, Principal Boyle."

She scowled. "I'm sorry?"

"I'm just glad *I'm* not the one who woke the ogre."

. . .

It turned out the mean, scary ogre Dad had been hiding inside him all these years looked just like normal, calm Dad. Which was kind of a letdown.

I thought Dad's dramatic exit meant he had a plan. I expected us to go over what our next move was in the car ride home. But we didn't. He stayed totally quiet, and I didn't know if that meant he was plotting or if he'd played his last card when he walked out on Boyle.

"I know I screwed up," I said, prompting him. "But two months is harsh. I know kids who did worse stuff than this and only got suspended a few days. They can't do this. Right?"

Dad didn't answer. I worried this was some kind of lesson. That he *wanted* me to worry that, yes, they could do this and there was nothing to stop them. But that had never been how Dad operated. Sometimes, he just needed to think.

That night, a story about my suspension ran on the local TV news. They interviewed Gray Suit, the school board guy who was in Principal Boyle's office. "The good news," he said to the reporter, "is that it appears there was, in fact, no sexual contact between the student and the teacher. This was just a case of a teen saying stupid things online."

I wanted to curl up and die. I couldn't believe this made the news.

My insta-friends had vanished. I tried texting Grant, DeShawn, and Lia for two days before my meeting at the school, and no one got back to me. The worst part was I didn't know if they thought they were blowing off a skizz, a liar, or someone who'd gotten suspended.

Before all this, I would have just gone on with my life. But I *needed* to know why they were ignoring me. They already knew I didn't sleep with Ashbury. They owed me an explanation.

Because of the suspension, I wasn't allowed in the school. So I hung out in the parking lot by Grant's beat-up Chevy until play practice ended. Just after 5:00, Grant, DeShawn, and Lia left the school. They were laughing and talking until they spotted me. Then everyone got quiet.

"Hi," I said, all smiles, like nothing could possibly be wrong.

Grant smiled back. "Hey, Jenny. Sorry to hear about . . . you know."

"Yeah," DeShawn said, "that's really crappy."

Both guys shifted from foot to foot. Lia just stared at the ground, her jaw clenched. She wouldn't even pretend she didn't want me there.

"I should have listened when you said to stay off The Confessional," I said.

Lia laughed, then quickly pursed her lips.

"How are you, Lia?" I asked warmly. After seeing Dad be bold and direct, some of it rubbed off on me.

"So," Lia replied, "is it true you're hanging out with Shaniece Burton now?"

I squinted at her. "What? Where did you hear that?"

"If you haven't figured it out by now, chica, word travels fast in this school. Heard you two were buddy-buddy in detention."

"Shaniece stuck up for me against some jerks," I said. "We just talked a little."

Lia rolled her eyes. "You know, I wanted to believe you when you said you didn't do anything with Ashbury. But now that I see who you're making friends with . . ."

Grant unlocked his car. "Jenny, it was good to see you but we gotta—"

I walked right up to Lia. She stood almost a foot taller than me, and I must have looked ridiculous staring her down, but that's just what I did.

"I guess maybe Shaniece is my friend," I said. "*She* stood up for me. That's what friends do."

Lia pushed past me and climbed into the passenger side of Grant's beater. DeShawn looked like he wanted to say something but thought better of it and crawled into the back seat. Grant and I stared at each other as he played with his car keys.

"Look, Jenny," he said, quiet so the others couldn't hear him, "I feel bad this is happening to you. I don't agree with Lia. But I also don't know what I can do to help. If you think of anything, let me know."

Then he hopped into the car and drove off. If he wasn't going to answer texts, he wasn't about to step up to the plate and do anything for me.

I was on my own.

CHAPTER TEN

I hadn't expected to see the Hmong Community Center decorated for Halloween. It's such a Western holiday, I never thought a place that works so hard to maintain our culture's traditions and values would embrace it. But Mee had told me that every so often, they let a little America in. "When in Rome . . ." Mee had said.

Dad was working late, so I snuck out and showed up at 7:00 for the Halloween party, dressed as a mummy. The place was packed. Monsters of every kind rocked out on the dance floor. I scanned the room, looking for Mee. All I knew was she had dressed as an astronaut.

I spotted Grandmother first, over by the punch bowl, chatting with the partygoers and handing out treats. Suddenly, it didn't matter that I'd been suspended. It didn't matter that the people I thought were my friends hadn't wanted anything to do with me. I still had my family.

I walked over to the punch bowl and tapped Grandmother on the shoulder. "Trick or treat, *niam pog*," I said.

Grandmother laughed and squinted at me. I unwrapped enough of the toilet paper I was using as bandages so she could see my face.

As soon as she realized who I was, she frowned. Teeth clenched, she started talking furiously at me, shaking her finger with every syllable. At first, I thought she believed I was someone else, so I quickly took off all the TP around my head. That only made her angrier.

"I don't understand," I tried to tell her. Her voice got louder, and people started to look our way.

I felt a hand on my shoulder and turned to find Mee. She was wearing a motorcycle helmet as part of her "space suit." She lifted the visor, and I could see she also was not happy. She said something to Grandmother, who immediately shut up but kept on fuming. Then Mee took me by the hand and led me away.

We stepped just outside the center. The sidewalk grew quiet as the music inside faded away.

"Does Grandmother not like mummies?" I asked. Maybe my costume was seen as disrespectful toward the dead.

Mee, who was usually all smiles, frowned. "What were you thinking, Jenny?"

"What do you mean?"

"I know about The Confessional."

I rolled my eyes. "Ugh, not you too. I already told you: I didn't sleep with Mr. Ashbury. The rumor you heard was wrong. You've got to believe me."

"It doesn't matter if I believe you. What matters is that you said it."

"It was a lie. I made it up. I promise."

"But you still said it. In Grandmother's eyes, it's just as bad as if you'd done what you said you did. You've brought shame to our family."

"Look," I said, "I'll go on the site and erase the comment. It'll be like it never happened."

Mee shook her head. "It *did* happen. You just don't get it, Jenny. Grandmother cried for two hours when she heard about what you said. She knows there's no way anyone can arrange a marriage for you now."

"Arranged marriage?" I asked. "You're joking, right? It's the twenty-first century. People don't still do that."

Mee looked like I'd slapped her across

the face. "It's rare, but those who stick to our traditions still arrange marriages, yes. We believe in family. I thought you did too. I thought that was why you were reconnecting with us."

"You thought I wanted someone else to pick a husband for me?"

"Family sticks together," she said, ignoring my question. "Everything we do affects the honor of the family. You brought us shame. It doesn't matter that you didn't sleep with your teacher. You said you did. That's what matters."

I didn't want an arranged marriage. I didn't know that I even wanted to stick with traditions. All I knew was that I wanted my family. They shouldn't have just given up on me like my so-called friends.

"Mee," I said, trying to sound calm, "please let me speak with Grandmother. I'll give her a week to cool off. Then I can come over and we can talk about this. I'll apologize. I'll do whatever she wants to make up for it."

For just a second, Mee appeared to be thinking about it. Like she felt sorry for me and would talk to Grandmother on my behalf. But that second passed, and her face clouded over.

"You should go home, Jenny," she said.

And she left me there on the steps of the center.

* * *

Dad didn't say a word when I came home. He should have reminded me I was grounded and extended my sentence. But maybe he could tell I'd been crying. So, instead of laying into me, he said, "We should talk about what comes next."

I threw off the rest of my toilet-paper costume. So he *had* been planning. I just didn't know if it would do any good. My own blood wouldn't stand by me.

"I don't know if I'm in the mood," I said, and started for my bedroom.

"I've been asking around," Dad said in a

tone that told me I wasn't going to be able to dodge him. So I stood in the hall just outside the living room. "We've got a couple options. First, you could transfer schools. I know that's not ideal, but it means you could continue the year with little interruption. It might be tricky getting another school to admit you, but we can try. Maybe we can get you into Mee's school, Madison North."

I shook my head. "That's really not a good idea."

Dad was good at reading me. Maybe too good. I didn't have to tell him that something had gone down with Mee. He could just tell.

"All right," he said, not pressing. "Let's talk option two. You make your case to the school board. The meeting to discuss you was an emergency meeting. Their next regular meeting is in a couple days."

I thought about standing up in front of a bunch of people like the stern-looking guy in the gray suit from Boyle's office. It definitely wasn't my favorite plan. But if there were only two options, I figured it was the one to go with.

"So how will that work?" I said.

"We get you on the agenda, and you can appeal their decision."

I'd never been much of a public speaker and I wasn't exactly thrilled with the idea of speaking to a room full of Gray Suits. "Can't we get a lawyer or something?"

"A lawyer would make this easier, yes. But we can't afford one."

"Can't *you* appeal the decision?" I asked. "They're more likely to listen to you. You sounded good going up against Boyle."

Dad took my hand. "I'll be right by your side. But this is something *you* need to do."

I hated the idea. *Hated* it. But I knew he was right.

"Okay," I said. "Let's do it."

CHAPTER ELEVEN

NOW
MONDAY, NOVEMBER 2

The one possible upside to the suspension was that I got to sleep in. Or, at least, I *should* have been able to sleep in. An unknown number texted me at the time I'd normally get up for school: *meet me in the food court at west towne mall at 7:00.*

I wrote back: *Who is this?*

i think i can help.

Which didn't answer the question. But at that point, I was willing to take all the help I could get. I threw on some clothes and hopped a bus to the mall. Only a couple restaurants were open that early, mostly serving breakfast. Sadly, my favorite milkshake place wasn't one of them. I sat down in the big empty court and waited.

It wasn't long before Shaniece Burton arrived. She stood over me, one hand on her hip. "Angry yet?"

"How did you get my number?" I asked.

"That skinny white boy who does plays gave it to me," she said. She meant Grant. "I asked you a question: are you angry yet?"

I shrugged. "Yeah, I guess."

Shaniece rolled her eyes. "I ain't got time if you only 'guess' you're angry."

She turned to leave, but I called after her.

"Wait, I'm sorry. I'm new at being angry. I don't have as much practice as you."

Her nostrils flared, then she burst out laughing. "Back talking me is suicidal, not angry. But it'll do." She handed me a roll of masking tape from her massive purse. "Come with me."

* * *

I couldn't believe it. Ten minutes later, I was following Shaniece into school.

"I'm not allowed here while I'm suspended," I said.

"First rule of being angry," she said, hooking her arm around mine, "is 'you gotta break a few rules.' Now, let's go wake people up."

We walked through the halls as students scurried around, getting ready for class. Shaniece pulled a handful of homemade flyers from her purse. Every few feet, I tore off a long piece of tape and she'd stick a flyer to the corridor wall.

"Listen up, Monona High," she yelled. "This here is Jenny Vang. You all know who she is. Did you also know she's been suspended for two months for saying she did something she didn't do?"

Hardly anyone glanced at the flyers. They showed an unflattering picture of me from my online profile under the word *UNFAIR* in all caps at the top. Next to me, it said: *Two Months. Lying.*

"Does that sound fair to you?" Shaniece continued. "Not me. It makes me angry. It makes me wonder how soon before they start handing out crazier punishments for small things."

A picture of a boy scowling at the camera sat under my picture on the flyer. Next to him, it read: *One week. Weapon.*

"Evan Miller got a weeklong suspension for bringing a knife to school," Shaniece said, pointing at Evan's picture on the flyer. "Five days for bringing a *weapon*. Think about that. And they want to kick Jenny out for two months."

The first bell rang, telling people they had five minutes to get to class. While most people continued to bustle past, a few stopped to give the flyers a read. Two more students were listed under Evan Miller. Each had gotten a lighter punishment than me.

I suddenly felt really guilty for ever judging Shaniece. She'd made these flyers on her own. Just to help me. Just because she knew what it was like to be treated unfairly.

"We've got to let them know that what they're doing is wrong," Shaniece told a pair of sophomores passing by. "Jenny doesn't deserve what she's getting. We gotta tell Boyle where we stand!"

We'd hung a dozen flyers at this point. But people were more interested in getting to class on time than listening. As Shaniece continued shouting, Grant appeared from around the corner, a stack of flyers under his arm. He thrust a flyer into the hands of anyone who ignored the ones posted on the wall.

A herd of students, heads down, rushed past us, like gazelles fleeing a lion. A second later, Principal Boyle followed in their wake. She walked right up to us.

"Take. Those. Down." Boyle pointed to the flyers. Shaniece glared defiantly for a second, then ripped the nearest flyer from the wall. I took down the next one. Grant grabbed the rest.

"You're not supposed to be here," Boyle said to me. Then she nabbed the rest of the flyers from Grant and Shaniece.

"We have the right to free speech," Shaniece said. "Just like Jenny had that right."

Boyle folded her arms. "If you didn't skip Civics so much, Miss Burton, you'd know there are limits to free speech. You can't yell 'fire' in a theater. And you can't say what Miss Vang said without expecting problems. You also can't hang posters on school property without the principal's permission. Which you *don't* have. Get to class now, and I'll forget this happened."

Shaniece sent her eye daggers into the principal's back as Boyle turned heel and disappeared around the corner.

"Thanks for trying," I said.

Shaniece shook her head. "Everyone's too scared. They don't realize Boyle can't punish us all if we stick together."

"People would listen if Boyle wasn't around," Grant said. "We need a way to rally everyone, but not at school."

I slumped against the wall. "It's hopeless. Boyle's only interested in teaching everyone a lesson."

"What do you mean?" Shaniece asked, eyebrows raised.

"It's something they said when they suspended me. 'If Jenny isn't punished, other students will think it's okay to make similar claims.' My suspension is a warning to stop anyone else from making false accusations."

Shaniece's eyes went wide. She looked at Grant and whatever idea had popped into her head popped into his too.

"It's crazy," Grant said, but it didn't sound like he believed it. "And risky."

"We can do it," she insisted.

They were making me nervous. "You guys wanna clue me in?"

Grant whipped out his phone. "Shaniece says Boyle can't punish us all," he said, his thumbs racing over the phone's screen. "I think we need to test that theory."

The bell rang, which meant Grant and Shaniece were late to class. But they didn't care. Together, they huddled over Grant's phone. I peeked up over Grant's shoulder and a chill crawled across my shoulder when I saw the bright red banner at the top of his browser.

The Confessional.

CHAPTER TWELVE

NOW
TUESDAY, NOVEMBER 3

I wore my nicest skirt with brand-new tights and pulled my hair back into a long ponytail. Dad wore a suit. We were waiting in the audience while the school board, seated at a long table at the front of the room, discussed issue after boring issue on their agenda.

There was a huge turnout. People were standing around the outside of the room. Word had gotten out that the skizz was going to try to defend herself. Parents wanted to hear what

I had to say for myself. Well, I couldn't wait for them to hear.

I kept an eye out for Grant and Shaniece. They were supposed to have arrived already. For one scary second, I worried that I really was on my own.

After half an hour, the board secretary mumbled that I'd come to appeal my suspension. He very nicely reminded everyone *exactly* why I'd been suspended, as if they'd forgotten. All eyes turned to me.

I stepped up to the podium and pulled the microphone down to my mouth. Five men and four women made up the board. I could see in their steely eyes that they'd already made up their minds. They were not repealing my suspension. So, basically, nothing I said would make a difference.

The anger Shaniece wanted from me boiled up inside. Whether they listened or not, I still needed to say what I came to say.

Gray Suit sat right in the middle, frowning

the heaviest. His nameplate told me he was *president* of the board. *Well, listen up, Mr. President. Angry Girl on deck.*

"Ladies and gentlemen of the board," I said, speaking directly into the microphone. "Forgive me for starting by stating the obvious: I screwed up. I'm new to Monona High and I was just trying to fit in and be like everyone else. But that's no excuse. I'm sorry for what I said and for any embarrassment I caused Mr. Ashbury or the school.

"That said, it's also important that you understand I am not being treated fairly. I made a false claim on an online message board. Supposedly, I violated the school's conduct code. If what I said online was a violation, I have to ask why I'm being singled out. Just a quick glance at The Confessional will show that *everyone* on there is violating the code.

"In case you didn't realize, you're in charge of a high school. Kids talk. You can't stop it.

Nothing you do to me is going to stop it. You want to make an example of me. Why no one else?"

I fell silent, waiting for the board to react. But no one moved, no one spoke. Then, Gray Suit cleared his throat.

"Miss Vang," Gray Suit said, "it's commendable that you've come here. You've spoken very eloquently. I was hoping you were coming to share your remorse with the board. Instead, you are attempting to defend the indefensible. You show no signs of understanding what I think should be the obvious lesson here: actions have consequences. If you're going to make false accusations about a teacher online, you need to face what follows." Gray Suit kept speaking as if nothing I said mattered, now or ever.

"You can't punish me for what I do on my own time outside of school," I said. "That's my father's job. He thought being grounded for a week fit the crime. A week. I've already spent nearly that in detention . . . for something that didn't happen in school. A two-month suspension is ridiculous. You're only using a past scandal as an excuse to let—"

Gray Suit actually banged a gavel on the table to shut me up. Which must have meant that I was winning. So I kept going.

"You're letting fear of what *might* happen interfere with giving the right punishment for what *did* happen. The punishment needs to fit the crime, and that's not what you're doing."

Out of the corner of my eye, I caught a slight—very slight—smile on the lips of old Stone Face Dad himself. He pointed to his heart and I knew what he meant. Turned out I had my own ogre inside and I didn't even know it.

"I think we've heard enough, Miss Vang," Gray Suit said loudly.

The doors to the board room opened. People standing at the back of the room parted as a river of students entered. Everyone was dressed sharply, playing the role of good little students. Leading the pack was Grant, wearing a suit, and Shaniece, wearing the tightest dress I've ever seen.

The students—dozens—spread out around the back of the room silently. Grant came right up to the podium and shook my hand. I moved away from the microphone as he stepped up.

"Ladies and gentlemen of the board," Grant said, straightening his tie, "my name is Grant Thomas. And I'm here to say that I had sex with Mrs. Krause, the drama coach. You know it's true 'cause it's on the Internet." He held up his phone, which showed The Confessional and the entry he'd made yesterday.

There was a distinct drop in cabin pressure as a hundred gasps echoed in the room. Then a boy I don't even know moved up next to Grant. "My name is Boyd Collins. And I had sex with Mr. Henson in the math department."

Boyd showed everyone his phone and his Confessional entry.

Every student in the room held up their phones. One by one, boys and girls stepped up to the mic and confessed imaginary sex with very real teachers. Gray Suit beat the table with his gavel, but even that didn't shut anyone up.

"I had sex with Mrs. Morrison, the librarian!"

"I had sex with Mr. Schieffer, the wrestling coach!"

Then Shaniece pushed her way up to the front of the crowd and grabbed the mic. "And, as anybody here will be more than happy to say, I had sex with all y'all!"

The room erupted in shouting. School board members huddled together, trying to figure out their next move. I stood on my tiptoes and whispered into Shaniece's ear. "You know," I said, "I think I'm going to get angry more often."

As Gray Suit fought to get everyone quiet, I glanced toward the back of the room. Just past the crowd, I could barely make out someone standing in the hall, just outside. As the figure leaned forward into the doorway, my stomach hit the floor.

It was Mr. Ashbury.

CHAPTER THIRTEEN

No one else saw Ashbury. Everyone was too busy arguing. But once I spotted him, I couldn't turn away.

Ashbury's gaze swept the room. He looked like he was going to be sick. When he got to me, our eyes locked. His jaw clenched, and after the longest five seconds of my life, he turned and left.

I pushed through the crowd of students. Most were still shouting the names of teachers they'd "had sex with." My insides squirmed as I raced out the door, down the hall, and into the parking lot.

Mr. Ashbury power-walked away, fumbling in the pocket of his blazer as he headed toward a white hatchback.

"Mr. Ashbury!" I called out.

He spun around and held up his arm. "Don't come anywhere near me," he said. Everything about his face—his narrowed eyes, his twisted mouth—said something completely different: *I hate you.*

"Mr. Ashbury, I want to apologize. I know you probably don't want to talk to me." I reached into my skirt pocket and pulled out an envelope. This was the apology I'd written. I'd planned to give it to the school board and ask them to pass it on to Ashbury. But now I knew I had to do this myself.

He stared at the envelope, then at me, like I was clinically brain dead. "I don't want to hear anything you have to say."

"What I did was stupid. I never let Principal Boyle believe it was true for even a second. As soon as she asked, I told her it was all made up. I even told the school board."

"Yeah," he muttered as he fished his car keys from his coat pocket. "I just saw your apology. Quite the rally. Are you proud?"

"What? No, I just—"

"Tell me something: what happens next? You've got your friends in there, crying wolf. You've won. You can all say whatever you want without any consequences because they can't punish you all. Well, what happens if a teacher really does take advantage of a student? You know it already happened. Who's going to believe a student who reports abuse now?"

My heart started hammering so hard I could feel it in my throat. That wasn't what this was about. This was supposed to prove . . . But it didn't. Not really.

"B-but," I stammered, "a two month suspension wasn't fair—"

Mr. Ashbury laughed. "Now you're going to tell me what's not fair? Yeah, that sounds about right. Well, you got what you wanted. You fit in now."

I felt like I was back in front of the school board, not being heard. But this time, my angry ogre failed me. It knew I was wrong. "No. It backfired, and now half the school thinks I'll sleep with anybody."

Ashbury threw his keys to the blacktop. "Oh, so this affected *your* reputation? Do you have any idea what your little prank cost me? I have been humiliated because of you. I have been treated like a criminal."

"I know and I'm sorry—"

"You know? Really? Please, Jenny, tell me what you know. Did you know that I was escorted from my classroom by two police officers, in front of all my students? Do you know they interrogated me at the police station for *five* straight hours? They didn't let me go until my boyfriend came to the station to swear that we've been a couple for the last three years."

His *boyfriend*? "I . . . I'm sorry. I didn't realize—"

"Well, now everyone knows. This was my first year here. I was going to let myself get settled, let people get to know me before I told anyone about my private life. Not all schools are gay-friendly. *You* took away my ability to do this on my own terms. *You* forced me to come out to save myself from going to jail."

I'd never seen anyone this mad before. Ashbury picked up his keys and opened his car door. When the dome light came on, I could see the inside of the hatchback filled with boxes and school books.

I held my breath, trying to hold in the tears. "What are those for?"

"I cleaned out my classroom. I resigned today, effective immediately."

"No! You can't do that."

"Already done. I want this over with. That's

why I didn't press libel charges. It just would have dragged this out. I'm ending it. Last thing I need now is for some guy to claim we had sex, just so he can boast to everybody. Do you know that's every teacher's worst nightmare? Being accused of something they didn't do." He glared over at the window where we could see the school board meeting, still in chaos. "And you just made it easier for that to happen."

I wanted to scream. I wanted to hit something. I couldn't even think straight. "I'm . . . so . . . sorry . . ."

I couldn't say anything else, because I was crying too hard. I just held out my apology letter at arm's length and prayed he'd take it. But he got into his car and drove off. I never saw him again.

CHAPTER FOURTEEN

NOW
WEDNESDAY, NOVEMBER 4

"The suspension's been lifted. You can go back to school tomorrow."

I stirred in bed that morning to find Dad standing just inside my bedroom. He handed out the news casually, like he'd just told me the sky is blue.

I should have jumped up and down. I should have squealed. I'd won. And it felt lousy.

"Did they admit the punishment was unfair?" I asked.

"Not in so many words," Dad said. "More likely, I think they realized they didn't have a legal leg to stand on. Someone may have threatened a lawsuit."

"You said we couldn't afford a lawyer."

"I said that to you. Not to them."

I nodded. I must have looked as sick to my stomach as I felt. Dad sat on my bedside and gave my hand a pat. I sat up and laid my head on his shoulder.

"Mr. Ashbury wouldn't accept my apology."

Dad sighed. "That'll hurt for some time."

He was calm, assured, and Stone Faced. As always. Sometimes that drove me nuts.

"So," I said, "what was all that stuff about an angry ogre inside you? All these years . . ."

"I used to be very angry," Dad confessed. "I argued with my family constantly. I didn't agree with what our culture demands, at least those bits that are upheld by the most traditional families. Like ours. Your grandparents disowned me when I married a girl they didn't approve of."

My mouth went dry. "Mom? You never told me that."

"I'm sorry," he said. "You were right. I grounded you partly because I was trying to protect you. I knew what your grandmother would do once she found out about The Confessional. I should have known it was going to happen sooner or later, no matter what I did.

"Our traditions work fine for many people. Just not me. I never wanted to rob you of your identity. That's why I brought us back to Madison after all these years. I had to give you a chance to decide for yourself if you wanted those traditions. You're old enough now."

I didn't know what I wanted. If I chose to honor our traditions, I was sure I could find someone at the Community Center to show me. But I had a lot of thinking to do first.

"Thank you," I said. "For supporting me if I honor our traditions. For supporting me through this whole mess. For everything."

He put his arm around me. We sat there, each with an ogre inside, waiting to get out. But not today. Hopefully, not for a long time.

. . .

I was on my third milkshake in the food court. The cleaning crews had started making their rounds. Any minute now, they were going to kick me out. The mall had closed five minutes ago.

I stared at my phone, trying to make it buzz. I'd sent three texts to Mee, begging her to respond. Telling her how desperately I need to talk to someone. But she hadn't responded and, deep down, I knew she never would.

"Was I right? She has an addiction to milkshakes."

I looked up to find Grant pointing at me. Shaniece was at his side. "We've been looking for you everywhere, girl," she said. "Answer a damn text, wouldja?"

Yes, my phone had been buzzing plenty.

Just not from Mee. She was the only one I'd wanted to talk to.

"I really want to be alone now," I said, slurping out the last bits of milkshake from my cup.

"When you ran out of the room last night," Grant said, "I followed you. I saw you talking to Mr. Ashbury in the parking lot. It looked ugly."

They sat down across from me, looking genuinely sympathetic. Giving up on Mee, I let it all spill out. I told them everything Ashbury had said. When I got to the part about how our demonstration at the school board meeting would make it harder for the administration to believe a student who really was being abused, they both got quiet.

"I thought we were helping," Grant said. "It . . . it made sense at the time."

"Last night," I said, "when I went to bed, all I could see was the guy from the school board's smug face, telling me that *actions have consequences.* He looked so satisfied when he said it, like it was something I didn't know. I knew, I just . . ."

"You can't take all the blame for Mr. Ashbury quitting," Shaniece said. "The school board could have stood behind their teacher."

"No, Shaniece," I said, "this is all on me."

No one said anything. Even with the mall closing, I couldn't even think about going home yet. Last night, I'd seen Gray Suit talking down to me. Tonight, I had a feeling that all I would see was Mr. Ashbury, driving away. I imagined a road that stretched out forever. No matter how long he drove, he could never get where he was going.

Grant and Shaniece each laid a hand on my arm. Somehow, I thought fitting in would feel better.

ABOUT THE AUTHOR

Gabriel Goodman is a writer living in St. Paul, Minnesota. He has written for other Darby Creek series including After the Dust Settled, Bareknuckle, and Surviving Southside.

SUSPENDED

THE CONFESSIONAL

A CUT TOO FAR

HIGH DRAMA

OVER THE TRACKS

TESTING THE TRUTH